TALES OF HONOR AND STRENGTH

Xavier Lamont Hall

Kenneth Maxwell Hall

ISBN: 979-8-9850310-1-0 (paperback)

ISBN: 979-8-9850310-0-3 (eBook)

Printed in the United States of America

DEDICATION

I dedicate this book to the people who shaped me into the person I am today and aided me in the creation of my book.

My family: Time and time again, my family did everything in their power to raise, protect, and support me. I would not have accomplished half of what I've done without them. I will always love my family.

My closest friends: These guys taught me so much about life and have inspired me to pursue knowledge and use my imagination to its fullest. I can't recall how many times they made me smile and laugh. I will always cherish my friends.

My 11th grade English teacher: This person is the reason why I became a writer. The lessons she taught me and stories she shared for class inspired me to use my imagination for the sake of writing. I will never forget her kindness and creativity.

I thank you all for everything.

TABLE OF CONTENTS

CHARACTER INTRODUCTIONS

Trinity: A vibrant and adventurous satyr, Trinity is someone who isn't afraid to tackle any challenge which comes her way. She upholds traditional values of her tribe, making her well-liked by her elders. She is also a strong role model for many of her peers. When the time comes for Trinity to prove her maturity, the elders give Trinity a mission as a rite of passage. Despite being told the mission is extremely dangerous, Trinity accepts it without hesitating. She is dedicated to proving herself as a satyr worthy of adulthood, in any way possible.

The Grim Reaper: Born as Brayonna Serrano, The Grim Reaper lives up to her name. A military veteran with a shady history, she is a freelance mercenary. Known for her ruthlessness, precision, and gritty attitude, the Grim Reaper is listed among the world's most dangerous individuals. Many military agencies have attempted to put down the Grim Reaper, but none prevailed. Eventually however, the Grim Reaper is given an unusual assignment; to train a squad of super soldiers assigned to the United States National Guard. Though she never considered herself a teacher, the freelancer is curious about this squad and accepts her assignment. What she does next is anyone's guess.

Agent Dakota: Being a Black Ops Agent is anything but an easy task. However, people like Agent Dakota are the exception. Ever since her birth, Dakota was an extraordinary person. Her skills and talents were admired and cherished by many people. Going as far as taking up military training at the age of three and graduating from college at the age of eleven. At the age of twelve, Dakota was given the chance to be a top tier soldier; she took it without a second thought. Dakota became the youngest and one of the most effective operatives the world has ever seen. Now, she fights side by side with her ally and friend Agent Firefly, learning as she goes.

A TALE OF HUNTRESSES

Trinity runs across the forest floor with haste. Her hands and hooves pound the ground with force, scooping up and tossing dirt and leaves behind her. Her body changes direction on a dime; leaping over creatures and dead logs with ease. At one point, she comes across a massive tree with multiple claw marks near its roots. Trinity realizes that she is on the right track. She takes a left turn and continues to run.

Later on, Trinity spots an identical tree and makes a right turn. Soon afterwards, she spots another identical tree and this time, proceeds to climb it. Her fingernails grow long and razor sharp just before she makes contact with the tree. She climbs faster than a squirrel, reaching the canopy in no time. Trinity sits on the tallest branch for a moment. She watches the ocean of leaves that surround her dance with the wind. She also sees over a dozen birds flying in formation to the south and a few monkeys leaping out of the canopies of other trees in the east. Trinity sniffs the air intensely. She catches a scent several miles southwest from her position. It is heavy with a reptilian odor and traces of blood from monkeys. "I know where you are, hunter," Trinity says to herself. She leaves the canopy, jumping down branch after branch with grace. Trinity reaches the forest floor and immediately resumes her run.

Time goes on as Trinity roams the forest, running through dense vegetation and avoiding environmental obstacles with impeccable agility. All the while relying on her sense of smell to guide her in whatever direction she chooses to go. Eventually,

Trinity stops in her tracks and stands before three massive trees bearing identical claw marks. These trees also bear a crude, circular carving above the claw marks that seem to represent the sun.

"This is it," Trinity thought to herself.

She walks in between the first and second trees and finds a dragon sleeping peacefully on a bed made of branches. Compared to Trinity's six-foot, six-inch stature and muscular build, the dragon herself was almost three times more physically impressive. The dragon's bluish gray scales are beautiful to see, despite many of them stained with blood. Her large wings rest just below her shoulders folded, whereas her long, slender tail constantly moves from side to side, brushing against the grass. Trinity is tempted to feel the dragon. She would have done so had she not educated herself with such a deadly creature. Trinity goes with a more direct approach of introducing herself.

"Tatsuya of Eastern Siberia!"

The dragon's ungodly yellow eyes pierce through Trinity's soul. Trinity doesn't move a muscle. The dragon raises her head from her bed, maintaining eye contact with Trinity.

"I am called Trinity. I come from a tribe of satyrs in the Northwest region of Siberia."

"I know your tribe..." Tatsuya's voice is deep and almost menacing. "The straightened horns on your forehead were a dead giveaway."

Tatsuya raises her hand and feels Trinity's horns. She is immediately fascinated with their stark thickness, as well as their finely sharpened tips. She can tell Trinity took care of her horns. As Tatsuya continued to feel Trinity's horns, she asks the satyr,

"You have reached maturity, correct?"

"Yes ma'am," Trinity replies with caution.

"Good..."

Tatsuya's hand moves from Trinity's horns to her face, slowly rubbing her cheeks and chin. Trinity remains motionless but shows no discomfort. The leathery skin on Tatsuya's hand is surprisingly soft and smooth.

"Why did you find me Trinity?"

"My elders sent me on a sacred hunt for three hobgoblins somewhere in Western Siberia. I have thirty-five days to find my targets and bring their heads back to my elders. They recommended I enlist the help of a dragon for this hunt."

"Not that I'm bothered by you coming to me, but why not seek the other dragons?"

Trinity thinks about her answer as Tatsuya moves hand from Trinity's face to her braided hair. Tatsuya finds it softer than silk.

"Each of the dragons in Siberia are unique, despite their similarities in power and tenacity. The dragon of Northern Siberia is a master of stealth and poison charms. The dragon of Southern Siberia is a master of illusions and deceit. The dragon of Western Siberia is a master of fire and black magic. You are a master of ice and lightning. The game I am hunting happens to abhor cold regions and avoids electrical storms."

Trinity sees a look of intrigue on Tatsuya's face. The dragon sits up from her bed, looking down on the satyr.

"Your logic is sound, Trinity. I must admit…the journey you seek to accomplish may be one I could enjoy. It has been a while since I have gone on a good hunt. But, what could you offer me if I choose to accept?"

"I offer the possibility of gaining the right to hunt near my region. There is a bountiful number of animals you could hunt at your leisure."

Tatsuya looks at Trinity for a moment. Trinity waits patiently for an answer. Tatsuya then holds her arm out to Trinity and a smile stretches across Tatsuya's face.

"I accept your request to accompany you on this journey."

Trinity smiles back and shakes Tatsuya's hand.

"I only ask you to trust me and I will trust you, Trinity."

"I will Tatsuya."

"Good."

Tatsuya rises from her bed, towering over Trinity like a tree. She talks a few steps back and gets down on her hands and feet. Her wings unfold and rest on the ground as Tatsuya looks back at Trinity.

"Hop on my back. I need to deal with someone before we leave. It won't be long."

Trinity's heart rate begins to accelerate. She has never before gone higher than the trees of this forest. She cautiously walks over to Tatsuya and gets on her back.

"I can tell you're afraid, Trinity. I'll take it easy on you for now."

"Th-thank you. I appreciate it."

Soon after that, Tatsuya jumps from the ground and begins to fly to the south. As promised, Tatsuya flies at a steady speed and stays just a few hundred feet above the trees. Trinity's anxiety somewhat lessens. Nevertheless, she keeps a tight hold on Tatsuya. Several minutes later, the duo flies near a small patch of trees that have been torn from the ground and they land at the center of it as gracefully as possible. As soon as Trinity touches the ground, Tatsuya looks at her and says,

"Tell me what you smell, Trinity."

Trinity smells the air around her. Her face immediately scrunches up in disgust.

"I smell trolls. Two of them. They must have come by here recently and destroyed everything in their way. They're close too."

"They came earlier today. I wanted to confront them when they entered my territory. How much do you know about trolls?"

"Not much, to be honest. I know trolls are quite strong and deceptively fast despite their bulk."

"Would you be bothered to fight trolls at this time? I think it would be an ideal opportunity to learn about each other."

Trinity thinks for a moment and shakes her head.

"No ma'am. I would not be bothered."

"Wonderful. Then lead the way, Trinity."

Trinity sniffs the air again and looks to the north. She runs in that direction with Tatsuya close behind her. Soon, the duo approaches a blockade of rocks in front of a huge ravine and hid behind this blockade. Trinity raises her head over the rocks ever so slowly and sees the ten-foot trolls in the middle of the ravine, gorging themselves on a pile of carcasses. The troll on the left has a reddish rash on its neck and chest. The troll on the right has large navy-blue circle tattoos on his arms and legs.

"Here's what we're going to do Trinity…" Tatsuya whispered to the satyr. "I'll confront the troll on the left and you take care of the troll on the right. I'll create a barrier between the trolls so that he has his undivided attention on you. But, be careful. When you have killed your troll, come to my aid as soon as possible. Do you understand?"

Trinity nods in response. She feels her heart rate slowly accelerate once again. Tatsuya senses Trinity's unease and places her hand on Trinity's. She whispers, "Trust me."

Tatsuya rises from the ground and with a deep inhale of air, she shoots an intense beam of magical ice at the trolls. A wall of ice rises between the trolls and the duo immediately confront the untamable beasts. A determined Trinity runs towards the tattooed troll and the latter is quick to react. It raises its arms to the air and brings them down upon Trinity; half a second too slow. Before the troll could recover, it stumbles back into the wall from an elbow strike by Trinity. The troll roars at the satyr and presses on its attack. It throws one punch after another at Trinity, who barely dodges each one. On one of the troll's punches, Trinity dodges it with great precision and lunges at the troll's arm before it can pull it back. The satyr sinks her razor-sharp teeth into the troll's triceps muscle and tears a rather big chunk of it off. The troll roars in pain, clutching its bloodied arm as Trinity spits out the piece of flesh.

"Disgusting," She says under her breath.

Before either the troll or satyr could do anything else, they hear the sound of lightning and turn to see huge sparks of electrical energy coming from behind the wall. Immediately after that, they see a stream of fire illuminated behind the wall, making contact with Tatsuya.

"That troll can breathe fire." Trinity thinks to herself.

As the troll turns its attention back to the satyr, Trinity slides under the troll, slashing in between its groin and right leg with her claws. The troll drops to one knee and Trinity immediately goes for its left leg. She completely tears off the troll's heel. The beast is now on both knees and in greater pain. Trinity hops on the troll's back and grabs hold of its face. The troll tries to shake off the satyr but that doesn't stop her from cutting its eyes. Trinity jumps to the ground and looks at the blinded troll, who clutched its nonexistent eyes with its uninjured arm. Trinity closes in on the troll and swings her arm just under the troll's chin. The troll's arm drops from its face and it struggles to take a breath. Trinity balls her fists up and repeatedly punches the troll in the face. Each punch knocks out teeth with relative ease. Trinity finishes off the troll with a powerful jab to the troll's nose, making it go into the troll's head. The troll falls to the ground face first, bleeding to death. Trinity then runs for the ice wall and climbs to the top in just a few seconds. Upon reaching the top of the ice wall, she sees Tatsuya holding off her troll with a barrage of lightning shooting from her fingertips.

As this is happening, Tatsuya and Trinity make eye contact and nod to each other. A moment later, Tatsuya ceases her barrage of lightning on the troll. The satyr jumps from the ice wall and towards the troll. The troll sees Trinity coming towards it but is unable to defend itself due to its fatigue from Tatsuya's lightning. With her left hand just above her head, Trinity lands a hit on the troll, nearly dislocating its lower jaw. Trinity lands on the ground with both hooves and quickly reengages the troll. This time, she jumps in the air and strikes the troll in the face four times with her hooves. After Trinity touches the ground, Tatsuya flies above her, head-butting the troll in the chest. The troll is sent flying through a spacious pocket of massive trees, crashing into one. The dragon and the satyr sprint towards the troll as it slowly gets back on its feet. Without hesitating, the troll grabs onto the tree, uproots it from the ground and turns it sideways. Now a makeshift club, the troll swings it at the duo at full force. Tatsuya and Trinity simultaneously punch the incoming tree, shattering it completely. The troll opts to use its fire breath. An intense stream of fire flies toward the dragon and satyr. Tatsuya protects Trinity with her wings just before impact. The troll moves closer to Tatsuya and Trinity, intensifying its flames with every step it takes. But, the dragon shows no sign of yielding. Neither does Trinity, despite not being able open her eyes from the intense heat.

As soon as the troll is a couple of feet from the duo, a huge mist of ice discharges from Tatsuya's body, covering everything around her within several hundred yards. The troll is now dazed and stiffened by the ice. Trinity isn't bothered much by the cold or the ice. As soon as Tatsuya curls her wings back, Trinity jumps toward the troll and punches it in the face. Tatsuya jumps in and punches the troll in the same area right after Trinity. Trinity strikes the troll again, this time with a kick to its temple. Tatsuya drives her knee into the troll's temple right after that. Trinity then jumps behind the troll and she and Tatsuya go for the troll's knees, dislocating both of them. Unable to stand, the troll sits helplessly as the dragon and satyr ruthlessly pound it from the front and back. At some point, Trinity grabs the troll by the arms and kicks its spine multiple times, destroying most of its vertebrae. Tatsuya drives her arm through its chest where its heart should be. The dragon unleashes a torrent of electrical energy within the troll, frying its internal organs and blacking its pale skin. The lifeless troll is then thrown to the side with its melted eyes looking up to the sky. The dragon and satyr stand face to face, smiling eagerly.

"This was fun. You handled yourself well, Trinity."

"Thanks. You were impressive too."

Tatsuya brushes off the blood on her arm while looking at Trinity.

"The troll you had me fight didn't have any powers?"

"No, it didn't Trinity. The only thing that it could do was amplify the powers of the troll who possessed magical fire. These trolls come from a populous tribe who practice this partnership. They are quite difficult to kill, unless their mystical connection is hindered."

"Ah. No wonder you wanted to create that ice wall."

"Yes."

"Also, you knew I could take the troll with no magic, even though I've never fought one before."

Tatsuya nods her head and replies,

"The strength and intellect your kind possesses are commendable. Both are much for a troll to handle."

"Wow. Then, this hunt may turn out to be great for both of us."

Tatsuya and Trinity walk away from the dead troll, side by side.

"What would you like to do next, Trinity?"

"I'd like to find some food. I ate a good portion of my rations on my way here."

"Very well. I know where to look."

BEHOLD THE GRIM REAPER!

"Alright everyone! Front and center on the double!"

Four soldiers wearing pale white shirts with green and black military trousers jumped up from the floor and quickly fell into formation, from tallest to shortest. Each soldier had a look of excitement on their faces and different weapons in their hands. The tallest soldier carried a genuine Viking era longsword. The second tallest soldier carried an authentic Japanese katana. The third tallest soldier carried a vintage Roman gladius and a circular, bulletproof shield. The shortest soldier carried a razor-sharp Ottoman Yataghan blade. I was the second tallest soldier. Standing before us was a mercenary codenamed The Grim Reaper. The mercenary's real name was Brayonna Serrano. She stood at five feet eleven inches tall; just three inches shorter than the tallest soldier of our unit. Brayonna wore the same kind trousers like the rest of us. She possessed a strong muscular frame. The kind heavyweight UFC fighters have. There were scars of varying sizes that covered almost every inch of skin on her arms and face. A testament to her resilience. Her weapon of choice was a double-edged light broadsword from the Medieval Europe era. The blade was sturdy and delicate. The hilt of the blade curved up on both sides in the shape of a "v". The handle was cylinder shaped, measured ten inches in length, and was completely clothed in black leather. I knew her blade was made by the very best blacksmiths.

"I hope you boys paid attention during training…"

Brayanna's voice echoed throughout the room with unwavering command.

"…because for the next nine days, your lives will be pushed to the brink of unbearable. You will be broken and rebuilt to become the soldiers your nation needs. If you give me any complaints regarding your tasks, I will push you harder. If you disrespect me at any time, I will hurt you. If you cannot keep up, I will have you sent back to basic training with fewer privileges and a new mentor who is just as stern as I am. Do you understand me?!"

"Yes ma'am!!"

My friends and I barked at the top of our lungs.

"Then let's get started. First on our list is a fencing session. What each of your files have told me is you are all able swordsmen. Each of you fight with different styles with your own set of strengths and weaknesses. I will give you two and a half minutes to stand your ground against me in one-on-one duels. If you last only for a minute, you will receive some of the more difficult tasks I have planned for you. Now… who wants to go first?"

The shortest soldier raised his hand the quickest. His name was Ian McCoy. He is the kind of person who can lighten the mood.

"Wonderful. Everyone else wait outside the ring."

We followed her command without a second thought.By the way, the room we were in was designed to allow us to safely and vigorously shape our skills in hand-to-hand combat. We use it five days a week, four hours a day. It hardly ever needs to be refurbished.

Brayonna and Ian shook hands with one another and they stood about three feet from each other. They unsheathed their swords and assumed their stances. Brayonna held her sword close to her neck with her left foot forward and right foot sideways. Ian angled his sword towards Brayonna and bounced back and forth like a boxer. For a moment, there was only silence. Everyone waited patiently for what could happen next. Another moment passed by and Brayonna yelled, "Begin!" Ian launched at her like a spring. For forty seconds, Ian was all over the place. His agility and acrobatic skills were three times better than Olympic gymnasts. His blade work was omnidirectional and ridiculously fast. If I were fighting him, he'd have caught me at least twice in those forty seconds. Not surprisingly, Brayonna held her ground. She used tight and efficient parries to meet most of Ian's strikes head-on and dodged everything else with impressive precision and timing.

Soon, Brayonna turned her defense into offense. Every time she parried a blow from Ian, she followed up with a blindingly quick sword thrust at his legs. Each cut slowed Ian down, making him strike more recklessly. To the best of my knowledge, Ian's legs were cut a total of seven times. It's possible Brayonna cut his legs more than seven times. But either way, Ian's legs became drenched in blood from his cuts. He couldn't keep up the pace. On one of Ian's downward strikes, Brayonna rolled to the side and kicked out with the bottom of her boot, hitting Ian in his rib cage. We heard two or three ribs shatter on contact and Ian tumbled back several feet away from Brayonna. Just before he could get back on his feet, Brayonna jumped on top of him and repeatedly welted him in the face. The sound of Ian's face shattering with every blow was almost too much to bear. Thankfully, Brayonna stopped herself from going too far. Ian's face was barely recognizable. He was dry wheezing rather than breathing regularly. I couldn't imagine how much pain he was in. It took Ian a minute or two to get back on his feet. As he barely stood before Brayonna, the first question that came out of his mouth was, "How long…did I last?"

"One minute and eight seconds." Brayonna replied.

"Thank you."

The third tallest soldier, Hector, helped Ian out the room. Brayonna then turned to me and the tallest soldier, Hamilton. She asked who wanted to go next. Hamilton raised his hand first. He and I met when we were in high school; he could be a video game designer if he wanted to.

"All right then Hamilton. Show me what you got."

"Yes ma'am."

Brayonna assumed her prior stance while Hamilton stood with his right foot forward and his longsword in both hands and pointed towards Brayonna. As soon as Brayonna shouted, "Begin!" Hamilton sprinted towards her with his teeth gritting and his hand choking his sword's handle. Unlike Ian, Hamilton attacked with strength-based attacks. He typically strikes with overhead cleaves and cross-cuts. Dueling with this man takes a harsh toll on one's stamina. Hector, Ian and I have learned this the hard way multiple times. However, that was not the case for Brayonna. While Hamilton's strength was apparently difficult for Brayonna to handle, she maintained a flexible and grounded defense. Not once did Hamilton's broadsword touch Brayonna. This went on for about thirty-four seconds. On the thirty-fifth second, Brayonna made her move. Instead of meeting Hamilton's strikes head on as she did with Ian, she began redirecting them. This allowed her to parry Hamilton's wrists rather than his blade, completely throwing off his momentum. As a result, Hamilton kept over lunging out of frustration. Then, Brayonna kicked Hamilton's blade from his hands and slashed him twice in the chest. Hamilton stumbled back in shock and before he could regain his focus, Brayonna slid under Hamilton's legs and sliced both his hamstrings. Hamilton let out a coarse yell and dropped to one of his knees. Then, faster than a lightning bolt, Brayonna attacked Hamilton with the techniques of Muay Thai and Kenpo. She used speed-based jabs and kicks to keep Hamilton disorientated and at bay. She used violently brutal elbow and knee strikes to whittle Hamilton down. He was no match for Brayonna's viciousness. His defeat was swift. The state Hamilton was in right after the duel was twice as bad as Ian's. He had suffered several broken bones and many bruises. Yet somehow, he didn't lose consciousness. As he rested, Brayonna knelt beside him and said,

"One minute and eleven seconds."

Hamilton managed to crack a weak smile.

"Thank you."

Brayonna then looked at me and asked,

"Rokutaro, is it?"

I nodded my head.

"Y-yes ma'am."

"Help your friend get to the medical bay and hurry back."

"Absolutely, ma'am."

It took me almost six minutes to run to the medical bay and back. The moment I stepped back into the training room, Hector and Brayonna had started their fight. I was so mesmerized by the duel I didn't even bother to step away from the door. It was like a chess match. Both fighters paid close attention to each other's movements and both struck one another at the best opportunity. It was relatively slow but exciting. Hector and I knew each other all the way from elementary school. He was a thrill seeker by heart and was always down for trying something new. On the subject of fighting, Hector always fought to outwit his opponents. Such a trait made him a strong leader for the team. Whether it was through offense or defense, Hector did not falter. He used his shield to meet sword strikes that were too quick for him to parry and welt Brayonna in any vulnerable portion of her body. He used his gladius to redirect Brayonna's strikes to off balance her and stab her in order to stay within her guard. I recall seeing Brayonna get stabbed at least five times and shield bashed seven times. I am certain of those numbers since speed was rarely ever Hector's strong suit. This chess match of a duel dragged on for a minute and twenty seconds. It was as good of a sign as any that Brayonna took this duel more seriously than her previous ones. However, as I had anticipated, the tide of the battle soon turned against Hector once Brayonna launched a counteroffensive. She was so ferocious, she made Hector look like an inexperienced child. I lost count of how many times he was stabbed and cut.

Hector was a hard bastard though. He endured the pain he suffered from as he waited for another opportunity. He did a good job too. In a last-ditch effort, Hector back flipped away from a cross-cut by Brayonna and just before he landed on his feet, Hector threw his shield at Brayonna's hands. To his luck, the shield knocked Brayonna's sword from her hands and Hector didn't hesitate to attack Brayonna once again. He integrated his blade work with his expertise in Shaolin Kung Fu, which was just as precise as his blade work. Brayonna steered clear of Hector's blade and took in his punches and kicks, allowing him to get close into her guard. When he got too close, Brayonna grabbed him by both of his arms and slammed her head into his nose. I saw Hector's nose cave in. Brayonna did not let up. She grabbed Hector's hand with the gladius and delivered a sharp uppercut to his lower jaw. The blow knocked the wind out of him. Brayonna twisted his arm and brought it over her shoulder, dislocating Hector's shoulder and elbow. The gladius was dropped to the floor and Brayonna threw Hector to the ground. He immediately held up his functional arm and shouted,

"I give! I give! I give!"

Brayonna helped Hector to his feet. She helped him calm down since he was in a great deal of pain. I ran over to help reattach Hector's shoulder. It took Hector several minutes to regain his composure. Once he did, Brayonna said to him,

"Two minutes and thirty seconds. Good work."

One look at Hector and Brayonna and I knew he felt ecstatic hearing her words but all he could muster was a choked up "thank you." He left the room after that and it was just Brayonna and me.

"Rokutaro, is it?"

"Yes ma'am."

"Show me what you can do."

"I'll do my best."

I hurried to the center of the room while Brayonna went to grab her sword. It was my moment to impress the Grim Reaper and I was nervously excited. I needed to be in a stable state of mind and Brayonna was kind enough to be patient. When I was ready, I looked Brayonna straight in her eyes and said,

"I'm ready."

Brayonna assumed her normal stance while I stood with my legs slightly bent, my right foot in front of my left foot, and my sword near my hip and the sharpened edge of the blade pointed to the ceiling.

After a few moments of silence, Brayonna herself launched at me without even saying "Begin." Her sudden change in approach, as well as her speed, was so jarring I reacted a second too late to block her overhead cleave; the blade left a huge gash across my chest. I stumbled back in shock and I received another two gashes in the same area. Then, Brayonna blitzed me with a right hook and I was sent to the ground, face first. I almost immediately jumped to my feet, while creating enough distance between me and Brayonna to prevent her from attacking again. In the next instant, I launched at Brayonna just as Ian did only this time, my movement was twice as fast and I attacked with incredibly fluid cross-cuts and stabs.

As I fought with everything I had to offer, my composure grew, which helped me overcome my pain. Suddenly, I began to enjoy the fight. For a moment, Brayonna was the one who was caught off guard and she was cut about four times. But, she soon became as stubborn as a brick wall; a brick wall reinforced with steel. Her blade blocked and parried my own with matching speed and superior precision. Even the couple of times I managed to cut Brayonna again barely slowed her down. I actually wasn't bothered by this. I have been waiting for a spectacular duel for years. Not that my friends were ever boring. I just needed someone else to fight for once.

After more than forty seconds of pure defense, Brayonna switched up her style. She added feints (deceptive blows) and ripostes (counter stabs) to her move set and used the full extent of her combative strength, speed and martial skill against me. Once again, her change of action was astute. My footwork became uneven. My speedy blade work became wild and sloppy. I suffered five broken ribs, both femurs bruised, several laceration and puncture wounds, and a dislocated knee; I fixed the latter though. I realized there was no way I could match her physical might and skill with my own. I had to answer my situation the best way I knew how; improvisation. It's how I have been able to keep up with and sometimes best my friends for the past twenty years. I subtly dubbed down on my boldness and began fighting in a slower, more calculated style. I was better able to anticipate Brayonna's sword sequence and fighting pattern. Using this to my advantage, I wielded my blade in ways none of my friends or even myself had ever seen. I also took the time to show off my skills in penchak silat. I had Brayonna on the ropes. She suffered from multiple lacerations, bone fractures, and contusions across her body. She struggled to maintain her guard. Feeling confident that I could finish the fight, I decided to transition from my slow and calculated approach to my preferred speedy and bold approach. Before I could do anything, suddenly Brayonna performed a one-handed backflip away from one of my cross cuts and swung her blade in an upward motion when I got close. I suffered another huge gash, this time on the left side of my face near my eye. I was completely thrown off balance again and then a second or two later, I felt blood running down my right shoulder and a searing amount of pain. Brayonna had jumped over my head and stabbed me in between my neck and right shoulder. Brayonna followed up with a sweeping leg motion, knocking me off the ground. She slammed the handle of her sword into my forehead. The blow was so strong it rendered my entire body inert. To my surprise, Brayonna dropped to the floor right next to me, just as exhausted as I was. I could tell that she too was done for the day. Brayonna got back on her feet several minutes later while I remained on my back. It was painful enough to take a breath. Brayonna looked down at me and replied,

"You're on the same level as Hector. Well done."

"Thank you."

Without another word, Brayonna swooped me up from the ground and carried me to the medical bay.

HOME INVASION

1 **300 Hours**

"HQ, this is Agent Dakota. We're less than a mile from our destination!"

A slingshot auto cycle roars down an empty road surrounded by densely packed trees. On this auto cycle are two masked individuals. They carry assault rifles over their shoulders with handguns and ancient blades on their belts. The driver holds a katana and the passenger holds a gladius.

"Copy that, Agent Dakota. Remember to proceed with caution. Judge Campbell and his associates must be terminated. The hostages must be saved."

The passenger raises her hand over her ear and presses into an earpiece.

"Will do HQ. We got this. Agent Dakota over and out."

A minute or two later, the shape of a two-story house appears in the distance. Upon seeing it, the driver turns to Agent Dakota and yells,

"We're getting close! Get the grenade launcher!"

Agent Dakota grabs a grenade launcher resting in between her and the driver. She opens it and verifies it is fully loaded.

"Once you see the vehicles…blow them all to Hell! I'll take out everyone else!"

"Copy that, Firefly!"

Soon, the agents find themselves several hundred yards from their destination. From this distance, they spot five pickup trucks parked in front of the house. Near these trucks are a dozen well-armed mercenaries; their faces covered with sunglasses and bandanas. Dakota takes aim with the grenade launcher and fires it four times. Each of the grenades land in between the trucks. An unholy hurricane of shrapnel and fire envelops everything it touches all for a few seconds. The agents pull up near the bloodied mess, leaving the auto cycle with their assault rifles in their hands. All that is left are smoldering piles of scrap metal and mutilated corpses. To their surprise, the agents find two mercenaries still clinging to life. True to his word, Firefly switches the safety off his rifle and puts a bullet in both of the mercenaries. Not even a moment later, the agents bolt for two wrecked vehicles a couple feet apart. As if on cue, a hailstorm of bullets rains down upon them. Firefly tilts his head up ever so slightly and sniffs the air. He looks at Dakota and shouts through his earpiece,

"I count eight bodyguards firing at us! Four on each floor!"

"I'll take the second floor!"

At the same time, the agents step away from their cover and return fire. With pinpoint accuracy, they land one headshot after another. In this exchange of fire, at least two of the mercenaries tag the agents with body and headshots before being killed. However, neither agent flinches from their injuries. In fact, the bullets, which had penetrated their skins, are forced out of their bodies.

"I'll go inside first!"

Agent Dakota shouts to Agent Firefly. Right after saying that, she rushes to the house and kicks down its double door entrance. They crash into three mercenaries at once, killing them instantly. Dakota spots seven more mercenaries near the entrance, shocked by her sheer power and frantically reach for their weapons. Dakota puts down four of the mercenaries in less than a second. As the remaining mercenaries discharged their weapon, Dakota finds a nearby piece of furniture unharmed from earlier and bolts toward it, not without receiving more injuries. Once she is behind it, Dakota takes her revolver out of its holster and uses it to land three headshots almost simultaneously. At this time, Dakota's injuries have healed and Firefly steps into the house. Firefly gives Dakota a look of disapproval and the latter responds with a shrug from her shoulders. Then, the sounds of boots and aggravated shouting echo from the second floor.

"I'll take point from here on out."

Agent Firefly asserted to Dakota. The agents carefully approach a staircase close to the end of the hall, which splits into two separate ones halfway up. Upon reaching the first few steps, three mercenaries on both ends of the staircase spot the agents and promptly shoot at them. The agents move much too quickly to be shot. The six mercenaries soon tumble down before the agents, with bloodied holes in their heads and torsos. The agents step over these corpses. Just as the agents poked their heads over the separate staircases, seven more mercenaries opened fire. Four mercenaries stand on one side while three stand on the other side. They use assault rifles and shotguns on the agents. The agents narrowly avoid being riddled with bullets and take cover. They remain in their positions for a moment until Firefly cues Dakota with a countdown of three seconds via hand gestures. As soon as he reaches the number one, he and Dakota rise up and fight back. In a flawless succession, the agents pick off their targets in mere seconds. They suffer a few more injuries in the process. Yet, the bullets do not cause them any discomfort. With the mercenaries dead or dying, the agents search each room top to bottom and find no trace of any of the hostages. Not one to be patient, Agent Dakota confronts one of the dying mercenaries. She shoves her hand into a rather large bullet wound just below his chest and squeezes whatever is beneath the skin. The mercenary screams in agony as Dakota stares at him disheartened.

"Tell us where the hostages are…"

She further tightens her grip on the mercenary's wound.

"…and I promise you won't suffer anymore."

The mercenary's screams soon transition into labored breathing. Tears pour out his eyes as if they were facets. Agent Firefly is less than pleased to watch.

"D-d-downstairs! There is a h-hidden door behind th-the stairway! O-old painting!!"

"Thanks."

As promised, Agent Dakota releases her grip on the mercenary's wound and uses her revolver to cover the floor with his brain matter.

"Let's find that painting."

Dakota says after shoving her revolver into her holster. It doesn't take long for the agents to find the painting the mercenary mentioned. Firefly cautiously sets the painting aside. In its place, a heavy metal door stands, locked by a key sequence via a button pad.

"I'll take it down."

Agent Dakota says while tossing her rifle over her shoulder.

"Try not to send the door flying. And we're using our blades and side arms this time."

"OK."

Agent Dakota lands three punches on the metal door. Each punch puts a huge dent into the door. Each dent is bigger than the previous one. Dakota finishes the job by delivering an elbow strike to the center of the door. The door comes off its hinges and it slides down the basement staircase. Once again, Firefly takes the lead. Upon reaching the end of the staircase, the agents find themselves standing before seven mercenaries and the disgruntled judge holding ten hostages at gunpoint. Half of the hostages are women.

"Isn't this typical?"

Agent Firefly says with disdain. The judge looks at Firefly right in the eye, cocks his pistol and replies,

"I'm only saying this once…"

Suddenly, eight gunshots echo throughout the room. The guns, which the judge and mercenaries have, are disabled by perfectly aimed shots. Everyone besides the agents are utterly shocked.

"Anyone who's tied up at the moment…"

Agent Firefly says as he presses on a watch on his left wrist, which begins to blink a blue light.

"…Go upstairs. We'll join you shortly."

Every hostage in the room immediately sprints upstairs. With the hostages out of the way, the agents turn their attention to the judge and the mercenaries. Shoving their side arms into their holsters, the agents unsheathe their blades. Firefly holds his katana with both hands and the blade near his temple. Dakota holds her gladius with her hand near the hilt and the blade pointed towards the enemy. One by one, the mercenaries fall victim to the agents' blades. On Firefly's end, his targets are left without their limbs and their heads. On Dakota's end, her targets are left with their throats slit and their bones shattered. All of this happens within seconds. Neither agent suffers any injuries this time. As the judge stands alone, now frozen with fear, Agent Dakota closes in on him. Faster than the judge could see, Dakota runs her blade through the judge's lower chest and follows up with a stab into the judge's heart. Blood pours out of his chest, ruining the black robe he wore for his profession. As soon as Dakota takes her blade out of the judge's chest, Firefly comes in, bringing his blade from over his head and down through the judge's torso. The judge's body drops to the floor in two pieces.

"HQ, this is Agent Dakota. Targets have been eliminated. Repeat, the targets have been eliminated."

"Excellent work team! You did a service to a lot of people. Your payment will arrive with your reinforcements. HQ out."

The agents wipe the blood off their blades and head for the first floor. On the first floor, the hostages huddle together next to a wall adjacent to the entrance, away from the entrance. Most of them wouldn't dare look at the aftermath that was all around them.

"Sorry about the mess."

Agent Firefly calls out as he and Agent Dakota walk towards the hostages.

"If you want, my partner and I can move the bodies to the basement."

The eldest of the hostages, who looked to be in her mid-thirties, nods her head and replies,

"Yes please."

The agents move around the room, pick up the corpses on the first floor and toss them down into the basement. The process takes a few minutes. Once they finished up, the agents approach the hostages once again and the eldest hostage says,

"Thank you."

"You're welcome."

Agent Dakota said with a smile. The second oldest hostage looks at the agents' tattered clothing. He asks the agents,

"How come your clothes have bullet holes and no bullets?"

Agent Dakota is quick to answer his question.

"We both recover from injuries much quicker and much more efficiently than the average person. How we gained this ability is classified."

"Oh…ok then."

The fourth eldest hostage is the second one to ask a question. Her question is directed to Agent Dakota.

"You look awfully young. Are you a teenager?"

"I turned thirteen a few months ago. But this is hardly my first mission."

The hostages exclaim in amazement.

"I have a question!"

The fifth eldest hostage says while raising his hand.

"Are you two mercenaries like the people you killed? Black ops maybe?"

This time, Agent Firefly answers the question.

"Black ops, yes. Mercenaries no."

"Pretty much. We hunt down any military or political official who needs to be arrested or killed."

"Is this a permanent job?"

"No. My partner and I are still figuring out what to do with our lives. This helps us pass the time."

"Huh. I guess I always figured people with your expertise would be willing to kill anybody for a good price."

"Life wouldn't be fun if everyone wanted you dead."

Agent Dakota states.

"Can't argue with that."

The fifth hostage says while rubbing his hair.

"I have a question as well…"

The eldest hostage starts. Her question is directed to Firefly.

"Why is your watch blinking like that?"

Agent Firefly replies,

"It has a tracking device. Our reinforcements will be arriving soon. Fifteen minutes tops."

The hostages nod and smile to one another.

"Does anyone else have a question?"

The seventh eldest hostage raises her hand enthusiastically.

"Are the people who are your reinforcements like you two?"

"Like us?"

Agent Dakota starts.

"No. They're ideal in taking care of people like you. And, to your point, there are other people around the globe who are like my partner and me. What they do with their time is their business."

The hostages "ooh" in unison.
"Okay, next question?"

The End